Ghost Girl

Written by
Katie Dale

Illustrated by
Jordan Kincaid

Chapter 1

"Ninety-eight... ninety-nine... one hundred! Ready or not, here I come!" Artie cried, uncovering his eyes and rushing out of the kitchen into the sunny farmyard.

Chapter Readers

'Ghost Girl'
An original concept by Katie Dale
© Katie Dale

Illustrated by Jordan Kincaid

Published by MAVERICK ARTS PUBLISHING LTD
Studio 11, City Business Centre, 6 Brighton Road,
Horsham, West Sussex, RH13 5BB
© Maverick Arts Publishing Limited November 2020
+44 (0)1403 256941

A CIP catalogue record for this book is available at the British Library.

ISBN 978-1-84886-732-1

www.maverickbooks.co.uk

This book is rated as: Grey Band (Guided Reading)

Where could Casey be hiding? He looked inside the stables, behind the tractor, then held his nose and checked the cowshed, but Casey wasn't there either. He hurried over to the barn, opened the door quietly and tip-toed carefully along the rows of hay-bales. Suddenly he heard a rustle in the next row! He grinned, then leaped around the corner.

"Gotcha, Casey!" he yelled triumphantly.

But it wasn't Casey. Instead, Artie found himself face to face with...

a ghost!

"ARGH!" Artie screamed. He ran out of the barn, raced across the farmyard, and slammed the kitchen door behind him, his hands trembling. The ghost couldn't get him in here, could she?

"Artie?" said a voice.

Artie screamed again and whirled round to face the empty kitchen. "Who... who said that?"

"Me," Casey said, crawling out from underneath the kitchen table. "Are you okay?"

"Casey!" Artie cried. "I saw a-a g-ghost!"

Casey's concerned frown turned to a glare. "Very funny. Is this your way of cheating at hide-and-seek? Because I still won."

"No, I'm not cheating!" Artie insisted. "There's a g-ghost in the b-barn!"

"Yeah, right, Artie." Casey folded her arms. "You can't frighten me."

"What's going on?" Mum asked, walking into the kitchen.

"Artie's making up ghost stories to try to scare me," Casey said, scowling.

"I'm not making it up!" Artie insisted. "I'll prove it! Come on!" He raced out of the kitchen.

Casey and Mum looked at each other, then shrugged and followed.

"Wait," Mum said, hurrying over as Artie reached the barn. "Let me go first, just in case there is something—or someone—in there." She stepped tentatively into the barn. "Hello? Is anybody in here?"

Everyone held their breath and listened carefully, but there was no reply.

They searched the whole barn, but there was still no sign of the ghost girl.

"See?" Casey said triumphantly. "No ghosts."

Artie frowned. He hadn't imagined the ghost, had he?

Chapter 2

After lunch, Artie decided to search the whole barn again to see if he could find the ghost girl. He took Sausage, their dog, with him to help him look. But there was still no sign of the ghost girl. Artie sighed heavily. Maybe he had imagined her.

"Woof!" Sausage barked suddenly, sniffing at a hay bale. "Woof! Woof!"

"What is it, boy?" Artie said, as Sausage scampered through the barn, sniffing the floor. Sausage led Artie out through the barn door, then suddenly broke into a run, yanking his lead free.

"Whoa, boy!" Artie cried as he chased after Sausage.

"Sausage, stop!"

But Sausage didn't stop. Instead, he raced across the farmyard, startling all the chickens and knocking over a bucket. Then he ran past Casey and into the stables.

"Oh no! He'll scare the horses!" Casey cried.

The horses stamped their feet and whinnied anxiously.

"Woof! Woof! Woof!" Sausage barked.

"Sausage, shhh!" Artie hissed, peering around the stables. "Where is he?"

"Over here," Casey said, spotting Sausage's wagging tail poking out of a stall.

"Woof! Woof! Woof!" Sausage barked.

"What are you barking at, boy?" Casey said, hurrying over to him.

Then she froze. For Sausage was barking at... the ghost girl!

Casey screamed—and the ghost girl screamed too!

Chapter 3

"What's wrong?" Artie cried, catching up. He gasped when he saw the ghost girl. He *knew* he hadn't imagined her!

Poor Casey had turned very pale—but not as pale as the ghost girl! Artie wasn't sure which of them looked more scared. But why would a ghost be afraid of people?

"I told you I wasn't making her up!" Artie whispered.

"B-but there's n-no such thing as g-ghosts..." Casey stammered.

"I'm not a ghost," the ghost girl said, cowering in a corner.

Artie frowned. "Then what are you? An alien? A monster?"

"No, I'm human, like you," the ghost girl said.

Casey frowned. "Then why are you see-through?"

The ghost girl sighed. "If I tell you, you must promise not to tell anyone else."

Casey and Artie looked at each other, then nodded.

The ghost girl took a deep breath. "I'm a time-traveller from one hundred years in the future."

Casey and Artie's jaws dropped.

"All time-travellers are translucent because we don't exist in this time period," she continued. "We're not supposed to be here really, and we mustn't change the past or we could affect the future."

"Wow!" Artie gasped. This was way cooler than seeing a ghost!

"I'm sorry I scared you both," the girl added.

"That's okay," Casey said. "I'm sorry I scared *you!* My name's Casey."

"And I'm Artie," Artie added.

"I'm L.E.," the ghost girl smiled, pointing to a name label on her jacket.

"L.E.?" Casey frowned. "Is that short for something?"

"I don't think so... I was named after my great-grandmother," L.E. replied. "My family have lived in this village for centuries, so we wanted to come back and see what it was like in the past. But everything's so different now. I got lost, and couldn't find my way back to my family or the time machine last night. I didn't know what to do or where to go, then it started to rain. Then I found your barn. It was open and dry, so I hid in there."

"It was open?" Casey frowned. "I thought you locked it after we played in there yesterday, Artie?"

"No, I thought you locked it!" Artie replied.

"I'm glad neither of you did!" L.E. said. "I don't know

what I'd have done if I'd missed my trip home *and* had nowhere to stay."

Casey gasped. "Your family left without you?"

"They had no choice," L.E. shrugged sadly. "The time machine can only stay in one time-zone for a few hours."

"But won't they come back for you?" Artie asked.

"Even if they did, they don't know where I am. And I don't know how to get to the meeting point," L.E. sighed. "I'm stuck here."

Casey and Artie frowned at each other.

"We'll help you get home," Artie said.

"Definitely," Casey nodded.

L.E. smiled sadly. "That's very kind, but there's no way to time travel from the past... and time-travellers can only stay in the past for two weeks."

"Why?" Artie frowned. "What happens after two weeks?"

L.E. swallowed hard. "We disappear."

Chapter 4

Casey and Artie were determined to help L.E.

They took her to stay in their caravan, which was much more comfortable than the barn, and took it in turns to sneak food to her. Artie winked at Casey as he slipped some extra fish fingers onto a napkin on his lap.

When he gave them to L.E. she nibbled one cautiously. "What is this?"

"Don't you have fish fingers in the future?" Artie asked.

L.E. looked astonished. "Your fish have *fingers?*" she gasped.

"No!" Artie laughed. "They're just finger-shaped pieces!"

"Oh, I see!" L.E. giggled. "Phew!"

"What's life like in a hundred years' time?" Artie asked.

"I... er... can't tell you," L.E. said. "I'm not allowed to tell you anything about the future, in case it changes anything. Sorry."

"Oh," Artie said, disappointed.

"But thank you for the fishy fingers!" L.E. grinned. "They're delicious!"

"You're welcome," Artie smiled.

When Casey brought L.E. breakfast on Monday morning, she also took her favourite books.

"We have to go to school today, and I thought you might be a bit bored on your own," Casey said, giving them to L.E. "So I brought you these."

L.E. stared at the books. "What are they?"

"Books!" Casey laughed. "Stories."

L.E. flicked through the pages, her eyes wide. "Amazing!"

Casey grinned. Life in the future must be very different.

She couldn't imagine a world without books!

Over the next few days, Casey and Artie researched time-travel. They looked online, in library books, and even asked their teachers. But they didn't have a time turner, a wormhole or a time machine, and L.E. had no idea how to make one.

As the days went by, L.E. grew sadder and sadder, and fainter and fainter. Soon she had read all of Casey and Artie's books, and was bored and miserable.

"I'll never get home," she sighed sadly. "It's hopeless."

"Poor L.E.," Casey said. "I wish there was something we could do to help her, or at least cheer her up."

"Me too," Artie said. "But what?"

They were out of ideas.

Chapter 5

The next morning, everywhere was covered in thick snow.

"School's cancelled!" Mum said, smiling. "Enjoy the snow! But make sure you wrap up warm!"

That gave Casey a brilliant idea.

She told Artie to keep their parents distracted for twenty minutes, and then meet her on the hill with the sledges. Then Casey gathered together all their warm clothes and took them to the caravan with some toast.

"Good morning, L.E.!" she cried.

"Is it?" L.E. muttered gloomily.

"Definitely," Casey grinned. She gave L.E. her snowsuit and wellies, Mum's ski goggles and woolly hat, and wrapped a big chunky scarf around her neck, nose and mouth. Soon L.E. was totally covered up.

"Now no one will know you're translucent!" Casey cried.

She poked her head out of the caravan. "Coast's clear!" she grinned, ushering L.E. outside.

L.E. gasped when she saw the snow. She bent down and touched it, then giggled.

Casey smiled. Maybe they didn't have snow in the future either?

She took L.E. to the best sledging hill in the village, where a crowd of children were already gathered.

L.E. was nervous at first, but no one noticed there was anything different about her.

"Told you it would work," Casey beamed. She showed L.E. how to make snow angels.

"This is fun!" L.E. giggled, waving her arms and legs through the powdery snow.

"Casey!" Artie puffed, running over with the sledges.

"I did as you asked." He glanced at L.E. "Who's that?"

Casey grinned. "It's L.E.!" she whispered.

Artie gasped. "Casey, you're brilliant!"

"Come on!" Casey beamed. "Let's go sledging!"

Casey and Artie showed L.E. what to do, and soon she was zooming down the hillside, whooping with delight.

"This is *amazing!*" she cried happily.

"Snowball fight!" someone yelled suddenly, and everyone cheered.

"Come on, let's join in!" Artie yelled, picking up a handful of snow. Soon everyone was throwing snow and laughing and ducking and squealing.

But then a big snowball knocked L.E.'s hat off, revealing her translucent head! She grabbed her hat quickly—but not quickly enough.

"Look!" a girl called Erica shrieked. "Her head is see-through!"

Everyone looked round as L.E. hastily put her hat back on.

"Don't be silly!" Artie said quickly. "Of course it isn't!"

"I know what I saw!" Erica cried, running up to L.E. "Take your hat off and show everyone!"

"No!" L.E. cried.

"Leave her alone!" Casey shrieked.

"Take your hat off!" Erica demanded, grabbing at L.E.'s hat.

"Get off her!" Artie pulled Erica away, and L.E. raced away through the snow.

"Come back!" Casey cried, running after her.

"She's a ghost!" Erica cried.

"Don't be stupid—ghosts don't leave footprints!" Artie said, pointing to L.E.'s tracks in the snow. "She's just shy and you scared her!"

He ran after Casey. They followed L.E.'s footprints through the snow, but as they entered a wood the snow disappeared, and so did L.E.'s footprints.

"L.E.!" they called, searching the woods. "It's okay now. We can go home!"

But L.E. didn't reply.

Artie and Casey called and searched for ages, but there was no sign of L.E.

She wasn't in the caravan either.

What if she was gone forever?

Chapter 6

The next day, the snow had melted, and Artie and Casey trudged to school miserably.

"I hope L.E.'s okay," Casey sighed.

"Me too," Artie said. "But even if we find her, if we can't think of a way for her to get home, she'll disappear soon."

"Poor L.E.," Casey said gloomily, as they headed to assembly. But instead of sitting in the hall as usual, the teachers ushered everyone outside.

"Today is a very exciting day!" the headmaster said when everyone had gathered on the field. "It is time to dig up our school time capsule!" Everyone watched as he dug up a metal box. "This was buried exactly fifty years ago today!" he continued excitedly. "Let's see what we've got inside!"

He opened the box, and held up the contents one by one. There was a letter, a newspaper, some old-fashioned toys, old coins, and photographs. "I bet life was very different then," he grinned. "And it will be very different in another fifty years!"

Suddenly Artie had an idea. He raised his hand.

"Can we make our own school time capsule?" he asked. "But this time let's bury it for one hundred years!"

"Yes!" The headmaster beamed. "What a wonderful idea!"

Everyone started chatting excitedly. Artie hurried over to Casey to explain his plan.

"We can write a letter to L.E.'s parents!" he whispered excitedly. "That way they'll get it in one hundred years, and know where to send the time machine to to pick her up!"

Casey's eyes shone with excitement. "Artie, that's brilliant! But what if it accidentally gets dug up early, or gets lost? We have to make absolutely sure it gets dug up at the right time." She raised her hand.

"Yes, Casey?" The headmaster said.

"Why don't we get the whole village involved?" Casey suggested. "We could bury it in the square and make a plaque so that it definitely gets dug up and opened at the right time."

"Great idea!" the headmaster said, smiling. "I'll call the mayoress and see what she thinks!"

That afternoon, the teachers told everyone that the mayoress had said yes! Casey grinned at Artie as they hurried home. They finally had a plan to save L.E.!

"All we need now is L.E.'s address," she said happily.

Artie's smile slipped. "But first we need to find L.E."

As soon as they got home from school, they took Sausage to the woods.

"L.E.!" they called. "L.E. where are you?"

"Woof!" Sausage barked, picking up a scent and running to a tree. "Woof! Woof! Woof!"

"Is it L.E.?" Casey said excitedly.

Artie peered up at the branches. "I can't see her," he frowned. "Sausage could be barking at a squirrel."

"Oh no!" Casey sighed. "What if we've lost her, just as we've finally come up with a plan?"

"That's it!" Artie said. "We need to tell her our plan!"

Artie and Casey shouted out their time capsule plan, then peered up at the tree. It still didn't move.

Suddenly there was a rustle behind them. It was L.E.!

"What a wonderful plan!" she beamed.

Chapter 7

Soon the whole village was buzzing with excitement about the time capsule. The mayoress arranged a special ceremony for the following Saturday, where she would bury the capsule, and then cover it in cement with a plaque saying the date it should be dug up.

"This is better than we hoped!" Casey said happily. "No one will be able to dig it up too early!"

"And just in time too!" Artie added. "On Saturday night, it will be exactly two weeks since L.E. got here!"

"Phew!" Casey said.

L.E. wrote and addressed the letter to her parents, telling them the co-ordinates of Casey and Artie's caravan, and asking them to come at ten o'clock on Saturday. She gave it to Artie excitedly.

"I don't know how I can ever thank you both enough!" she said, her eyes sparkling. Casey and Artie grinned.

But when they got to school, they had a horrible shock.

"I know everyone wants to put something in the time capsule," the headmaster said in assembly. "But now the whole village is involved, there just won't be room. So we will put in one item from each class. On Friday, each class will vote for their favourite."

Casey and Artie looked at each other anxiously. What if their classes didn't choose L.E.'s letter?

"Let's ask L.E. to write a second letter!" Artie said. "Then we'll have two chances to get it into the time capsule."

"Great idea!" Casey nodded. So L.E. wrote another letter, and they each took one in.

Over the next few days, everyone brought in a variety of items for the time capsule and Casey and Artie got more and more nervous.

Finally Friday arrived. Casey crossed her fingers as her class voted... but they chose a doll! She hoped Artie had more luck.

Artie crossed all his fingers and his toes as his class voted... but they chose a class photo!

"No!" he cried. "It's not fair! The time capsule was my idea, so my letter should go in it!"

"I'm sorry, Artie," his teacher said. "But the class has voted."

Artie sighed. He had to do something! Then he had an idea.

"Can I at least take the photo to the headmaster?"

"Yes," his teacher smiled, handing it to him.

Artie grinned. He picked up L.E.'s letter too. Once outside the classroom, he slipped the photo into his bag and gave L.E.'s letter to the headmaster's secretary instead! Hurray!

But when Artie and Casey arrived home, Mum was cross.

"Artie, I've just had a phone call from your headmaster," she said. "He says you switched your class's time capsule item and put your own letter in instead. Is this true?"

Artie flushed bright red. "Yes. I just..." he hesitated, but he couldn't tell Mum the truth—he'd promised L.E. he'd keep her secret. "I just really wanted my letter to go in."

"Well it hasn't," Mum said crossly. "The headmaster is very angry and so am I."

"I'm sorry," Artie said miserably.

"You are grounded until you have finished all your homework and all these chores." Mum gave him a list.

"But Mum!" Artie cried. "It's the burying ceremony tomorrow! I can't miss it!"

"No buts!" Mum said crossly. "I'm very disappointed in you, Artie."

Artie's shoulders slumped as he trudged to his room.

"What are we going to do?" Casey said anxiously, following him. "We've got to get L.E.'s letter in the time capsule before it gets buried, or she'll never get home!"

"You'll have to do it," Artie said. "L.E.'s counting on you."

Casey gulped.

Chapter 8

The next day, Casey hurried to the village square early, hoping to slip L.E.'s letter into the time capsule before everyone arrived, but the village was already bustling with people. The mayoress was there, holding the time capsule, and didn't put it down for a single moment. Gradually the square filled with people, then finally the mayoress picked up a microphone.

"Welcome to the time capsule burying ceremony!" she beamed.

Everyone cheered. Except Casey. She had to do something, quickly!

"Stop!" she cried, pushing through the crowd. "Stop!

My doll's in there!"

The mayoress looked up, concerned.

"Please don't bury her!" Casey begged. "I changed my mind! I need her!"

The mayoress sighed, smiled, then opened the box.

Casey knocked it to the floor, spilling the contents everywhere.

"Careful!" the mayoress cried.

"Where is she?" Casey said, rummaging through the items, while secretly pulling L.E.'s letter from her pocket. She just had to slip it in without anyone noticing...

"Casey!" a sharp voice cried. "Stop!"

Everyone looked round as Casey's teacher stormed forward.

"I'm sorry, mayoress, that doll doesn't belong to Casey," he said. "It's fine to put it in the capsule. What were you thinking, Casey?!"

"I... I'm sorry!" Casey sighed as he ushered her away. That was her one chance—and she'd blown it.

"No!" Artie cried, watching the ceremony online on his bedroom computer.

Casey had got so close to putting the letter in! He wished he could go and help her, but even though he'd been up since the crack of dawn doing his chores and homework he had a whole short story still to write before he was allowed out.

Mum knocked on his bedroom door. "Everything okay?" she asked, looking in.

"Um, fine," Artie said, quickly closing the webpage. "I just realised I've been misspelling something all morning."

"Never mind, that's what spell-check's for," Mum smiled, walking in with a sausage sandwich. "I thought you'd like some lunch. You've worked really hard this morning. I'm amazed how quickly you've done all your chores—and I loved your short story you printed downstairs earlier! How did you pick your main character's name? That's how I used to spell my name sometimes, you know?"

Artie frowned, confused. He hadn't even started writing his short story yet, unless... L.E. must have written it for him!

"How're you getting on with your homework?" Mum asked. "Nearly done?"

"Just finished!" Artie beamed, grabbing his sandwich and rushing out the door. "Thanks, Mum!"

He fetched Sausage and ran to his bike. He'd have to

cycle quickly if he was going to get to the ceremony in time!

"Woof!" Sausage barked, jumping up at something. "Woof! Woof!"

"What is it, boy?" Artie frowned. He couldn't see anything.

"It's me," L.E.'s voice said quietly. "I'm invisible. I don't have long, Artie. I can feel myself fading away."

Artie gasped. "Then we'll have to hurry! Climb on my saddle. Let's go!"

Artie put Sausage in the basket and pedalled as fast as he could, hoping against hope that they weren't too late.

Chapter 9

Casey watched helplessly as the mayoress put all the spilled items back in the time capsule, placed the capsule into the hole, and gave a long speech. Finally, she covered it with soil.

"Ladies and gentelemen, our time capsule is buried!" she cried. "Now, it's time to seal it!"

The workmen approached with the cement.

"Let's count down!" The mayoress cried happily. "Ten! Nine! Eight..."

Casey felt her heart sink lower with each number.

"Seven! Six! Fi—" suddenly the mayoress's microphone stopped working. She tapped it, frowned, and held up a hand to stop the workmen. What was going on?

Just then, Sausage hurtled through the crowd, and jumped straight into the time capsule hole!

Casey gasped. What was Sausage doing here?

"Woof!" Sausage barked, soil flying everywhere as he dug up the time capsule. "Woof! Woof!"

He jumped out—with a sausage in his mouth!

"Shoo, dog!" The mayoress snapped. "Shoo! Shoo!"

"Woof! Woof!" Sausage replied, gobbling the sausage then jumping up at the mayoress and tripping her up!

Suddenly, Casey felt L.E.'s letter being pulled from her hand—but there was no one there! It must be L.E.!

"Shoo, doggy! Shoo!" the mayoress snapped, as Sausage sniffed at her pocket—and pulled out another sausage! "How did that get there?" she gasped.

Casey giggled.

"Whose dog is this?!" the mayoress demanded.

"Mine!" Artie called from the back of the crowd. "Here, Sausage!"

Sausage bounded through the crowd towards Artie, knocking everyone out of the way.

"No, he's mine!" Casey cried. "Here, Sausage!"

Sausage changed direction and ran towards Casey, knocking into more people.

"Here, boy!"

"No, here!"

Sausage hurtled back and forth through the crowd as Casey and Artie called him in different directions.

"Someone catch that naughty dog!" the mayoress cried. Everyone tried to catch Sausage as he raced this way and that, slipping through their fingers, knocking things over and causing a huge commotion.

Everyone was so distracted they didn't notice the time capsule lid opening, or a letter slipping inside.

"Someone catch that dog *NOW!*" The mayoress boomed loudly as her microphone suddenly clicked back on.

Artie caught Sausage and gave him another sausage from his sandwich. "Good boy! Good job!"

"Now, let's *finally* bury our time capsule!" the mayoress huffed, straightening her dress. She hastily piled the soil back on top and nodded at the workmen. "Three, two, one, go!"

As they poured the cement on, everyone cheered— especially Casey and Artie!

Chapter 10

That night Casey couldn't sleep. At five to ten, she tiptoed into Artie's room. He was already on his window-seat, peering out at the caravan. They smiled at each other.

"Do you think it worked?" Casey asked nervously.

"Only one way to find out," Artie patted the seat next to him, and Casey hurried over as the clock struck ten o'clock.

"I wonder what a time machine looks like!" Artie whispered excitedly.

They peeked out at the dark farmyard. Everything was still.

"Was that dustbin always next to the caravan?" Casey frowned.

"I'm not sure…" Artie said.

Just then, the caravan door opened and closed.

"It's L.E.!" Casey hissed.

As they watched, the bin lid lifted off silently, and a light shone from inside, lighting up L.E.

"The bin must be the time machine!" Artie gasped.

L.E. looked up at their window and grinned. Then she held a finger to her lips.

Artie and Casey zipped their mouths shut and smiled.

Silently, L.E. climbed into the dustbin and closed the lid on top. The light went out, and the bin disappeared.

"We did it!" Artie beamed.

"I'm so glad she's going home!" Casey grinned. "But I'll really miss her. I wish we could see her again someday."

"Me too," Artie nodded.

"We don't even have anything to remember her by," Casey sighed.

"Yes we do!" Artie said, running to his desk.

"The short story she wrote for my homework!"

They read it together. It was a story about a girl called L.E. who time-travelled from the future and was helped by two wonderful friends, R.T. and K.C.

"She thought our names were initials too!" Artie laughed.

"L.E." Casey smiled. "Like Ellie."

"Like Mum," Artie said. "She said she used to spell her name like that sometimes too."

Casey and Artie looked at each other.

"L.E. said she was named after her great-grand-mother..." Artie said.

"And her family come from this village..." Casey added. "Could one of us be L.E.'s grandparent?"

Artie grinned. "Maybe we *will* see her again one day..."

Discussion Points

1. What did Artie and Casey put in the time capsule to help L.E.?

2. Who found L.E. in the barn at the beginning of the story?

a) Artie

b) Casey

c) Mum

3. What was your favourite part of the story?

4. What was the time machine disguised as at the end of the story?

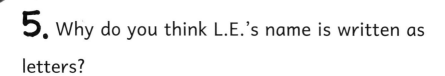

5. Why do you think L.E.'s name is written as letters?

6. Who was your favourite character and why?

7. There were moments in the story the characters had to **solve problems**. Where do you think the story shows this most?

8. What do you think happens after the end of the story?

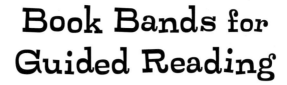

Book Bands for Guided Reading

The Institute of Education book banding system is a scale of colours that reflects the various levels of reading difficulty. The bands are assigned by taking into account the content, the language style, the layout and phonics. Word, phrase and sentence level work is also taken into consideration.

The Maverick Readers Scheme is a bright, attractive range of books covering the pink to grey bands. All of these books have been book banded for guided reading to the industry standard and edited by a leading educational consultant.

To view the whole Maverick Readers scheme, visit our website at

www.maverickearlyreaders.com

Or scan the QR code to view our scheme instantly!

Pink
Red
Yellow
Blue
Green
Orange
Turquoise
Purple
Gold
White
Lime
Brown
Grey

Maverick Chapter Readers
(From Lime to Grey Band)